Returning to Colombia

CRABTREE
PUBLISHING COMPANY
WWW.CRABTREEBOOKS.COM

Linda Barghoorn

CRABTREE
PUBLISHING COMPANY
WWW.CRABTREEBOOKS.COM

Author: Linda Barghoorn

Editors: Sarah Eason, Harriet McGregor, and Janine Deschenes

Proofreader and indexer: Wendy Scavuzzo

Editorial director: Kathy Middleton

Design: Paul Myerscough and Jessica Moon

Photo research: Rachel Blount

Production coordinator and Prepress technician: Ken Wright

Print coordinator: Katherine Berti

Consultant: Hawa Sabriye

Written, developed, and produced by Calcium

Publisher's Note: The story presented in this book is a fictional account based on extensive research of real-life accounts by refugees, with the aim of reflecting the true experience of refugee children and their families.

Photo Credits:
t=Top, c=Center, b=Bottom, l= Left, r=Right

Cover: iStock: andresr

Inside: Shutterstock: A7880S: p. 16l; F. A. Alba: p. 7t; Steve Allen: p. 9l; Andreas Wiking Andersson: p. 11c; Ernesto Aponte: p. 14b; Kristopher Blais: p. 16; Chipmunk131: p. 1l; Daisyx: p. 6tr; Benoit Daoust: p. 22b; DavidBautista: p. 7; Bumble Dee: p. 22t; Sebastian Delgado C: p. 23; Drogatnev: p. 25r; Elenabsl: pp. 20b, 27cr; Gcafotografia: p. 26t; Hanohiki: p. 27c; Jiw Ingka: p. 23cr; IsoVector: p. 18br; Ruslana Iurchenko: p. 15; Ivan_Sabo: pp. 6b, 20; Helga Khorimarko: pp. 3, 18bl, 19b, 21cr; Kolopach: p. 4t; Jess Kraft: pp. 6t, 12-13t, 26b; Lawkeeper: p. 23t; Light_s: p. 16t; Loveshop: p. 5cl; Macrovector: pp. 11b, 22bl; Yannick Martinez: p. 14c; Ekaterina McClaud: p. 19; Mspoint: p. 28t; Nowaczyk: p. 18; Parose: p. 14t; Posztos: pp. 24, 28b; Johasir Rivera: p. 21cl; Paul Stringer: p. 5cl; Sudowoodo: p. 29t; Barna Tanko: pp. 5r, 8; Watch The World: pp. 12b, 25; What's My Name: pp. 12t, 15t; John Wollwerth: p. 1bg; Murat Irfan Yalcin: p. 27r; © UNHCR: © UNHCR/Fabio Cuttica: pp. 10-11t; © UNHCR/Siegfried Modola: p. 29c; Wikimedia Commons: José Camilo Martínez S: p. 13b.

Library and Archives Canada Cataloguing in Publication

Title: Returning to Colombia / Linda Barghoorn.
Names: Barghoorn, Linda, author.
Series: Leaving my homeland: after the journey.
Description: Series statement: Leaving my homeland : after the journey | Includes index.
Identifiers: Canadiana (print) 20190114614 | Canadiana (ebook) 20190114665 | ISBN 9780778764984 (softcover) | ISBN 9780778764861 (hardcover) | ISBN 9781427123725 (HTML)
Subjects: LCSH: Refugees—Colombia—Juvenile literature. | LCSH: Refugees—Ecuador—Juvenile literature. | LCSH: Refugee children—Colombia—Juvenile literature. | LCSH: Refugee children—Ecuador—Juvenile literature. | LCSH: Refugees—Social conditions—Juvenile literature. | LCSH: Colombia—History—1974-—Juvenile literature. | LCSH: Colombia—Social conditions—Juvenile literature.
Classification: LCC HV640.5.C7 B37 2019 | DDC j305.23086/91409861—dc23

Library of Congress Cataloging-in-Publication Data

Names: Barghoorn, Linda, author.
Title: Returning to Colombia / Linda Barghoorn.
Description: New York : Crabtree Publishing Company, [2019] | Series: Leaving my homeland: after the journey | Includes index.
Identifiers: LCCN 2019023010 (print) | LCCN 2019023011 (ebook) | ISBN 9780778764861 (hardback) | ISBN 9780778764984 (paperback) | ISBN 9781427123725 (ebook)
Subjects: LCSH: Refugees--Columbia--Juvenile literature. | Refugees--Ecuador--Juvenile literature. | Refugee children--Columbia--Juvenile literature. | Refugee children--Ecuador--Juvenile literature. | Return migration--Columbia--Juvenile literature.
Classification: LCC HV640.5.C7 B373 2019 (print) | LCC HV640.5.C7 (ebook) | DDC 362.7/791409861--dc23
LC record available at https://lccn.loc.gov/2019023010
LC ebook record available at https://lccn.loc.gov/2019023011

Crabtree Publishing Company
www.crabtreebooks.com   1-800-387-7650

Printed in the U.S.A./082019/CG20190712

Published in Canada
Crabtree Publishing
616 Welland Ave.
St. Catharines, Ontario
L2M 5V6

Published in the United States
Crabtree Publishing
PMB 59051
350 Fifth Avenue, 59th Floor
New York, New York 10118

Published in the United Kingdom
Crabtree Publishing
Maritime House
Basin Road North, Hove
BN41 1WR

Published in Australia
Crabtree Publishing
Unit 3 – 5 Currumbin Court
Capalaba
QLD 4157

What Is in This Book?

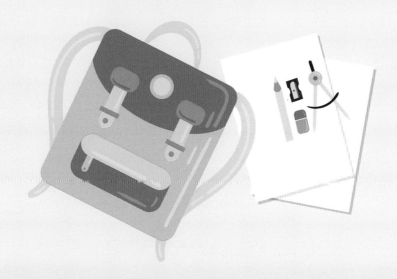

Andres's Story: Dreaming of a New Home

Hola, hello! My name is Andres. I grew up near the city of Pasto in Colombia. My family has lived on the land there for many generations. We are farmers.

When I was nine years old, my family had to leave Colombia. People were fighting against the government. They were part of the **rebel groups**. The war started many years before I was born. The fighters wanted more **rights** for the Colombian people. Things got worse and worse. The rebel groups were fighting against one another, too. They each wanted control of the country. They demanded money and land from people, and said they would hurt them if they refused. They even forced children to be soldiers. No one was safe.

Costa Rica

Caribbean Sea

Panama

Colombia is in the northern part of South America. Its capital city is Bogotá.

Venezuela

Pacific Ocean

Bogotá

Colombia

Pasto

Ibarra

Ecuador

Brazil

UN Rights of the Child

You have the right to live in a country where your government protects its **citizens** from war, **poverty**, and **discrimination**. While you read through this book, think about these rights.

Colombia's flag

Ecuador's flag

Ibarra is a busy market town in Ecuador. It is a two-hour drive from the Colombian border.

For a long time, the fighting was far from our village. We all tried to live a normal life, but we were always nervous. We hoped the war would not come closer. But, when the rebels arrived in our village, our lives changed forever. We had to flee to Ecuador. Now we live in a city called Ibarra. We are safe, but people do not want us here. We do not feel welcome. We miss Colombia and want to return home.

My Homeland, Colombia

Colombia is a beautiful country. It has tropical rain forests, mountain ranges, and a long Pacific Ocean coastline. More than one-third of the country's land is used for farming.

Colombia's **civil war** began in 1947. For many years, poor farmers had been treated badly by the wealthy landowners they worked for. When the farmers asked their government for help, the government refused. So, the farmers formed rebel groups to fight the government for better rights and freedoms. FARC (the Revolutionary Armed Forces of Colombia) was the most powerful of the rebel groups. It wanted to control all of Colombia. Landowners formed groups to defend themselves against the rebels.

The war lasted more than 50 years. Thousands of people were killed and millions were **displaced** from their homes. In 2016, the Colombian government offered a **peace deal** to FARC to end the war.

Bogotá is home to more than 10 million people. The Andes Mountains rise behind it.

Many people fled their villages during the war and were forced to live in slums in large cities such as Bogotá.

These people are protesting in Bogotá to demand peace.

Not everyone wanted to end the **conflict,** however. During the war, FARC had controlled the trade of illegal drugs. They made a lot of money. New rebels wanted to take over the illegal drug trade. So, they continued to fight each other for control. FARC leaders discussed the peace agreement with the government. FARC agreed to end the conflict. In exchange, it demanded a role in the government so that it could take part in making decisions about the country's future.

Story in Numbers

During the long conflict, more than

200,000

people were killed. Around

6.5 million

Colombians were displaced.

Andres's Story: Thinking of Home

From our small apartment in Ecuador, Father watched the news of the peace agreement closely. He wondered if peace would last. He looked for signs that it might be safe to return home. He felt it was safer to wait and see what would happen.

Mother really wanted to go home. She knew that life in Colombia was still uncertain. It had been five years since my brother, Diego, was taken from us by FARC. They wanted him to be a soldier. Mother refused to give up hope that we would see him again. She said a prayer for him every night at dinner. She wanted to continue the search for him in Colombia.

These women are selling local foods in a market in Ibarra. Corn is an important part of many Colombian meals.

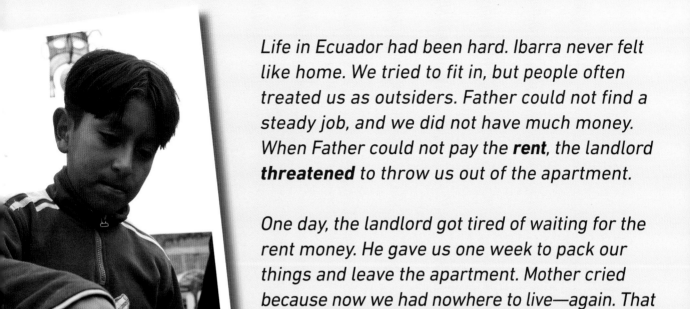

*Life in Ecuador had been hard. Ibarra never felt like home. We tried to fit in, but people often treated us as outsiders. Father could not find a steady job, and we did not have much money. When Father could not pay the **rent**, the landlord **threatened** to throw us out of the apartment.*

One day, the landlord got tired of waiting for the rent money. He gave us one week to pack our things and leave the apartment. Mother cried because now we had nowhere to live—again. That was the day Father decided to return to Colombia. He said there was nothing left for us in Ecuador.

This boy sells snacks in a local market in Ecuador. Children often work to help support their families.

Andres's journey began in Pasto, Colombia. He and his family first traveled north to Bogotá. But when life there became unsafe, too, they went south to Ibarra in Ecuador.

Story in Numbers

Approximately

54,000

Colombian **refugees** live in Ecuador. About one in four of these are children.

Bogotá

Colombia

Pasto

Ibarra

Ecuador

A New Life

Since the peace agreement was signed, the Colombian government and FARC have tried to make plans to rebuild the country. But it has been difficult to make a plan that everyone can agree on. The government promised to pay for programs that would help people reclaim land that was taken from them and to rebuild their homes. But things are moving slowly, because there is not a lot of money to spend. Citizens have become frustrated. They are eager to rebuild their lives and the country.

The war is officially over, but there is still violence by rebels and **gangs** in some areas of Colombia. Since 2015, refugees from Venezuela have arrived in Colombia. They are in need of food and safety. The Colombian government must now take care of them as well as its own **internally displaced persons (IDPs).**

These Venezuelan refugees wait for a meal prepared by volunteers in Colombia. They fled their country because its economy collapsed. People did not have money to survive there.

Medellin, in northwest Colombia, saw some of the worst violence during the war as rival gangs there fought for control of the local drug trade.

Most Colombian refugees are reluctant to return home. They do not think the peace agreement between FARC and the government will last. Colombian refugees who choose to return home are warned by aid organizations that it is still very dangerous in their homeland.

Andres's Story: Coming Back Home

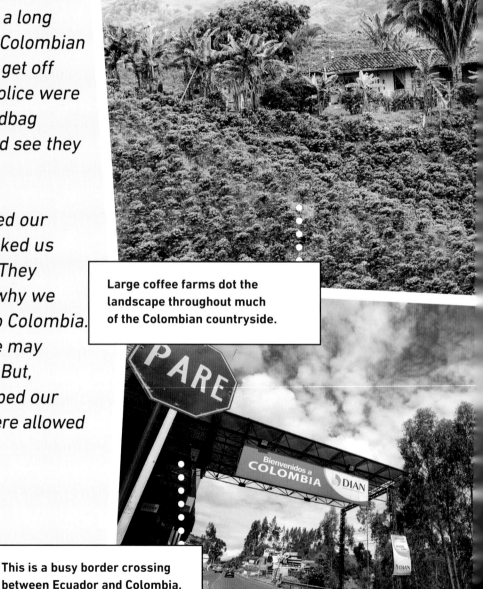

Soon after Father's decision to leave, we boarded a bus. It was going to be a long ride home. At the Colombian border, we had to get off the bus. A lot of police were there, behind sandbag **barricades**. I could see they had guns.

The police checked our passports and asked us many questions. They wanted to know why we were returning to Colombia. They said that we may not be safe here. But, finally they stamped our passports. We were allowed to pass.

Large coffee farms dot the landscape throughout much of the Colombian countryside.

This is a busy border crossing between Ecuador and Colombia.

May 4
Dear Journal: We are finally going back to Colombia! We are nervous about what will happen in the days ahead. But we are hopeful for new beginnings. I wonder what our farm will look like after being abandoned for so long.

We passed through many villages. The countryside looked so peaceful. Mother and Father began to sound more hopeful. In the seat behind me, I heard them discuss plans to visit the government office in Pasto. Father wanted to apply for some money. It would help us get our farm running again.

In one village, we passed a government sign that said, "Together, peace and life after the conflict are possible!" But it was covered with many bullet holes. That made me very worried.

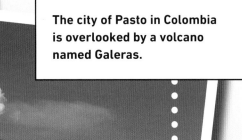

The city of Pasto in Colombia is overlooked by a volcano named Galeras.

Story in Numbers

It is estimated that less than

5%

of all Colombian refugees have returned home each year since the peace agreement was signed.

A New Home

Since the war ended, the government has tried to **resettle** IDPs. It built houses for them in crowded slums in or near cities. Living in slums is difficult. Basic services are not always available, and people living in poverty are sometimes forced to commit crimes to make money. But many IDPs live in slums because they feel it is safer than living in the countryside, where many rebel groups operate.

The government also wants to teach former FARC rebels how to return to normal life. But the FARC rebels have been soldiers for many years. They have seen terrible violence, which often causes emotional challenges such as **PTSD**. Due to their past, many former rebels face discrimination and are refused jobs or housing. It is very difficult for them to leave their past behind.

Families living in slums like this one in Bogotá often find themselves trapped in poverty. With limited access to jobs and education, it is difficult for them to improve their lives.

Many Colombians who fought in the war were badly wounded. They need good health care to recover, but proper health care is not available in many places in Colombia.

You have the right to live in a clean and safe environment where there is safe water to drink, **nutritious** food, and proper health care.

Children living in crowded slums often have few safe places to play outdoors.

New government programs promise returning refugees that they will get their land back. But many new landowners refuse to give the land back, even if it was stolen after the refugees fled. The government also promises money to returning refugees, and to bring health care and education to areas once controlled by the rebels. But there is not enough money to make this happen. Change is slow.

Andres's Story: My New Home

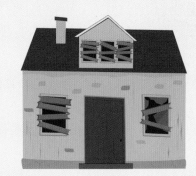

It was strangely quiet when we arrived in our village. I saw faded graffiti covering many of the village walls. They were written by FARC soldiers and had threatening messages. Some of our neighbor's houses looked abandoned. I wondered if they were refugees, too.

The front door of our house was broken. Someone had forced their way in. Some of the furniture was missing or broken. Mother's garden was buried under an enormous tangle of weeds. Father held Mother as she cried. Our home was ruined. None of us slept well that first night home.

Refugees often lead very vulnerable lives in crowded slums.

Story in Numbers

More than **25,000** square miles (64,750 square km) of land, about the size of the state of West Virginia, was abandoned or stolen during the war.

Traditional farmhouses were often made of adobe (mud) brick. This kitchen contains only the basics for cooking.

*Early next morning, Father went to the government office. He wanted to apply for a **grant** to help rebuild our farm. He returned home with good news. He filled in a form to prove the land is ours. He hopes the government will approve it. That means they agree that we own our land. The government has also promised us money. Mother has contacted a local church organization. They help reunite families with former soldiers. They will try to help us find Diego.*

June 12
*We are home! The government has promised Father money for seeds and farming tools. But not everyone in the village is as hopeful as Father. Many complain that they have not received the money promised by the government. They are thinking about planting coca. It is used to make the illegal drug **cocaine**. They can earn much more money with coca than by growing vegetables. But Father refuses to grow it. He says, "Where there is coca, there will be gangs and violence."*

17

A New School

Most young children in Colombia go to school, but education is very different in different parts of the country. Some schools in larger cities have enough money for good education programs. These schools enjoy well-trained teachers, computers, sports equipment, and clean classrooms. But in poorer parts of the country, schools do not have enough money. Many schools do not have supplies or Internet access. The government has promised money toward improving education, but progress has been slow.

Students at city schools often have access to better education than those in village schools.

UN Rights of the Child

You have the right to a good quality education that will enable you to pursue your goals.

Rural schools often do not have enough teachers. Because many rural areas are still controlled by gangs, teachers fear violence. They are also paid very little. Roads that are badly maintained can make it impossible for cars or school buses to travel on them. They may even become flooded or washed out during heavy rains. This can make it hard for teachers and children to get to school.

Without a proper education, children from poor, rural communities will have fewer chances for healthy, successful lives as adults.

Land mines left over from the war are still in the ground. This makes the journey to school even more dangerous. Active rebel groups still recruit children to work in the drug trade delivering packages, acting as lookouts, and collecting drug payments. They promised the government they would stop, but they have not.

Some poor families cannot afford for their older children to go to school. Students stay at home to work and support their families.

Andres's Story: Learning at Home

Mother and Father worry about our education. They did not know what education we would receive back in our village. Father thought maybe we could live in Bogotá for a while. He said schools there have more money and better teachers. But Mother remembered how unhappy and afraid we were in Soacha when we lived there. She refused to live in a big city again.

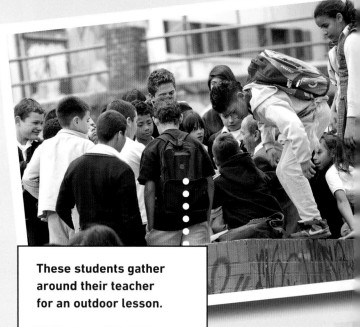

These students gather around their teacher for an outdoor lesson.

Our school needs many repairs, and there are few supplies for us to use. The principal is frustrated. He told my parents that the government always promises that the money is coming soon. But it never does.

Story in Numbers

On average, students in more wealthy areas of Colombia attend school for

12 years.

Students in poorer, rural areas attend school for only

6 years.

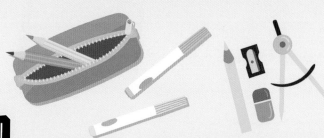

Many of my old teachers were threatened by the FARC soldiers. FARC tried to recruit them. Some of them fled and have not returned. Two new teachers arrived last week from a city far from here. Mother worries how long they will stay. I am more worried they will not teach us properly. Their lessons have not been good so far. But, we have had the most amazing news this week, too!

This worn patch of earth is a playground outside this school. Money for outdoor play and sports equipment is hard to find.

Hola Mateo!
I am sending this message from one of the school computers that is not broken. We returned to Colombia last summer after we could not afford the rent on our apartment in Ecuador. I am back at school, but will have to work hard to catch up. You will never believe the best news, though. We just found out that Diego is alive! Now we are waiting for him to come home to us. Your friend, Andres

Everything Changes

The government faced difficult choices in its agreements with FARC. The group saw itself as a defender of citizens' rights. It demanded a voice in Colombia's future. In exchange for peace, the government promised FARC a role in running the country. The government also promised to **pardon** former FARC members for crimes they had committed as soldiers if they promised to stop fighting and returned to their communities peacefully.

During the war, many people saw their homes destroyed and family members killed by FARC. They could not forgive the former rebel soldiers. They believed it was wrong for FARC rebels to be pardoned of war crimes. They did not want FARC to have a role in the Colombian government.

This soldier wears the FARC badge on his uniform.

Many Colombians fear police violence **and** corruption.

Protestors demonstrate against government corruption. The sign in front reads, "Colombia is tired of corruption."

VOTE

In 2018, a new Colombian president was elected. He wanted to build a strong economy and reunite the country. He promised to tackle the corruption that was crippling the country. Money promised by the former government for important education, health, and housing projects had been wasted or not delivered. Criminals went unpunished by a legal system that does not work properly.

Many people remain fearful and uncertain. Gangs still control some parts of the countryside. Citizens protesting peacefully for more rights and freedoms have been beaten and even killed by corrupt police. These police want to stop any kind of demonstration against the government. They do not want the people to have a voice in deciding Colombia's future.

Andres's Story: My New Way of Life

At long last, Diego returned to us last week! A volunteer named Gabriel from the church organization brought him home to us. Gabriel will work with Diego. He will help him adapt to life back in our community. Tomorrow, he will take Diego to be enrolled in a training and education program. Then he can find work.

To help former FARC rebels return to normal life, they are given a monthly wage and help finding a first job such as in construction or street cleaning.

Story in Numbers

In 2017, more than

12,000

former FARC soldiers returned to their communities to begin new lives.

Some of the villagers stared as Diego returned. They looked suspicious. Many suffered badly under FARC. Mother says they want to see every FARC soldier punished. They have little room in their hearts for forgiveness. I wonder how we will build a new country without forgiveness. And how will these people treat Diego now that he has returned to us?

Hola Mateo!
You will never guess who has come home!
Yes, it is Diego! Mother has been crying
happy tears for weeks. But not everyone in
the village is excited to see Diego return.
Some want him punished for belonging to FARC.
Why should Diego be punished for being taken
away against his will? Your friend, Andres

Many of Colombia's elders worry about the future of their country.

Father wants to know why the government
has not approved the form that will let us
own our land. He is still waiting for the
government money he needs to buy his farm
tools. Last week, he planted the lettuce
and red pepper seeds the government sent.
He hopes to sell the vegetables in Pasto. But
he will need to find more work to support us.

Andres's Story: Looking to the Future

Diego has found a job in Pasto. He works three days a week in a small store. But it has been hard for him. Many people do not want to give jobs to former FARC soldiers. People in our village still do not trust Diego. Mother worries about the effect this has on Diego. His emotions are very up and down. Father wonders whether we should move somewhere else. We could go some place where no one knows about Diego's past.

Children find relief from the Colombian summer heat in a city water park.

Festivals and carnivals are an important part of life in Colombia. These dancers perform at a festival in Barichara, one of Colombia's historic towns.

UN Rights of the Child

You have the right to your own individual identity, which no one can take away from you.

Soccer is the most popular sport in Colombia. People play it almost anywhere! This field is actually a street in a town in northern Colombia.

Gabriel continues to help Diego. He visits our family regularly. Diego is working so hard to move forward. But I think it will take many years for my brother to recover from the time he spent as a FARC soldier. I hope we do not have to move again. Our land form has finally been approved. The farm is ours! We have started to build a life here again.

*Volunteers from the United States have come to my school. They introduced an athletic program called Sports Without Borders. It is trying to encourage students to stay in school longer. I am excited about the sports classes. There is a ton of new equipment coming! I want to practice my English with the American volunteers. I hope I can graduate from high school one day. Maybe I can go to university. I want to be a lawyer who fights for **equality** and opportunity for every citizen. I want to make Colombia a country we can be proud of.*

Do Not Forget Our Stories!

Many refugees dream of returning home. They want the lives, family, and friends they have left behind. They can play an important role in rebuilding a homeland devastated by war and poverty. Their children can be educated to become the next generation of leaders. They can try to bring safety, equality, and freedom.

The war in Colombia is over. The government is eager to create a new, more hopeful country. Much of the world has turned its attention to other areas of conflict. But violence and extreme poverty are still part of daily life for many Colombians. Colombia needs the world's help. It is working hard to bring peace to all its citizens.

These Colombian citizens are enjoying an afternoon out in the historic center of Bogotá.

UN Rights of the Child

You have the right to live with dignity in a society that guarantees your freedom.

Venezuelan refugees are fleeing government corruption and shortages of food and medicine.

While Colombia looks to the future, its neighbor, Venezuela, is in conflict. Colombians once fled to Venezuela for safety. But Colombian refugees are now taking Venezuelan refugees into their homes. They have offered food, shelter, and medicine to new refugees in need of help.

There are many conflicts across our planet. Many refugees' stories are never heard. But each refugee is a person with an important story to be told.

Discussion Prompts

1. What are some of the challenges faced by Colombian refugees returning to their homeland?
2. Why are some Colombians angry about how former FARC soldiers are treated?
3. What could the Colombian government do better to support IDPs and refugees in their homeland?

Glossary

barricades Temporary walls or structures to prevent someone from entering a place

citizens Persons who belong to a country and have the right to that country's protection

civil war A war between groups of people in the same country

cocaine An illegal drug

conflict Fighting

corruption Dishonest behavior by someone in a position of power over others

discrimination Unfair treatment of someone because of their race, religion, ethnic group, or other identifiers

displaced Forced from the area where they live

economy The system in which goods are made, bought, and sold

equality The state of having the same rights as others

gangs Organized groups of criminals

grant Money or land that is given to someone by a government

internally displaced persons (IDPs) People who are forced from their homes during a conflict but remain in the country

land mines Explosive devices that are placed underground

nutritious Containing substances needed to keep healthy

pardon Forgive a crime

peace deal An agreement that formally ends a war

poverty The state of being very poor, making little money, and having few belongings

PTSD Post traumatic stress disorder; an anxiety disorder caused by distressing events

rebel groups People who fight against a government

refugees People who flee from their country to another due to unsafe conditions

rent Money paid to live in someone's house or apartment

resettle Settle in a new place

rights Privileges or freedoms protected by law

rural Relating to the countryside

slums Makeshift housing in which very poor people live

threatened Promised hurtful actions to get someone to do something

Learning More

Books

Hudak, Heather C. *Immigration and Refugees* (Get Informed—Stay Informed). Crabtree Publishing Company, 2019.

Roberts, Ceri. *Refugees and Migrants*. BES Publishing, 2017.

Wallace, Sandra Neil, and Rich Wallace. *First Generation: 36 Trailblazing Immigrants and Refugees Who Make America Great*. Little, Brown and Company, 2018.

Wiseman, Blaine. *Colombia* (Exploring Countries). Av2 by Weigl, 2016.

Websites

https://kids.nationalgeographic.com/explore/countries/colombia/#colombia-dancing.jpg
Learn more about Colombia's history, people, and culture.

www.therefugeeproject.org
Delve into the global refugee crisis through facts and figures.
Click on Colombia to learn more about refugees and current news.

www.unhcr.org/teaching-about-refugees.html#facts
UNHCR's website provides reliable online facts and figures about refugees, migrants, and IDPs.

www.unhcr.org/uk/news/videos/2016/7/577a86304/colombia-owning-a-home.html
Watch this movie about displaced persons in Colombia.

Index

About the Author

Linda Barghoorn studied languages in university because she wanted to travel the world. She has visited 60 countries, taking photographs and writing stories about the people and cultures of our planet. At home, she volunteers at a local agency that provides newcomers and their families with clothing and community support.